PIPER GREEN *and the* FAIRY TREE

PIPER GREEN and the FAIRY TREE

ELLEN POTTER *Illustrated by* QIN LENG

Alfred A. Knopf

New York

THIS IS A BORZOI BOOK PUBLISHED BY ALFRED A. KNOPF

Text copyright © 2015 by Ellen Potter
Jacket art and interior illustrations copyright © 2015 by Qin Leng

All rights reserved. Published in the United States by
Alfred A. Knopf, an imprint of Random House Children's Books,
a division of Random House LLC, a Penguin Random
House Company, New York.

Knopf, Borzoi Books, and the colophon are registered
trademarks of Random House LLC.

Visit us on the Web! randomhousekids.com

Educators and librarians, for a variety of teaching tools,
visit us at RHTeachersLibrarians.com

Library of Congress Cataloging-in-Publication Data
Potter, Ellen.
Piper Green and the fairy tree / Ellen Potter ; Qin Leng. — First edition.
   pages cm. — ([Piper Green and the fairy tree ; 1])
Summary: "Piper's older brother leaves Peek-a-Boo Island and
Piper refuses to take off his old earmuffs, no matter what! Things are
going from bad to worse . . . until she discovers the Fairy Tree."
   —Provided by publisher
ISBN 978-0-553-49923-0 (trade) — ISBN 978-0-553-49924-7 (lib. bdg.) —
ISBN 978-0-553-49925-4 (ebook) — ISBN 978-0-553-49926-1 (pbk.)
[1. Separation (Psychology)—Fiction. 2. Brothers and sisters—Fiction.
3. Family life—Fiction. 4. Schools—Fiction. 5. Islands—Fiction.]
I. Leng, Qin, illustrator. II. Title.
PZ7.P8518Pip 2015
[E]—dc23
2014025814

The text of this book is set in 17-point Mrs Eaves.
The illustrations were created using ink and digital painting.

Printed in the United States of America
August 2015
10 9 8 7 6 5 4 3 2 1

First Edition

Crow Island

Egg Isla[nd]

Mink Island School

MAINLAND

MINK ISLAND

CHAPTER
ONE

THE IMPORTANT STUFF

There are two things you should know about Peek-a-Boo Island:

1. All the kids on the island
   ride a lobster boat to school.

2. There is a Fairy Tree
   in my front yard.

I have a lot of other things to tell you too. My brother Erik says I should start with the most important stuff, though. He is fourteen and very smart.

If you don't like lobster boats or Fairy Trees, you should probably do something else. For example, you can go outside now and look for beetles. My little brother, Leo, likes to do that. He only eats the green ones. He says they taste like bacon.

CHAPTER TWO

EVERYONE LOVES MONKEYS

It was the first day of school. When I sat down at the table to eat breakfast, I was wearing my new orange shirt and a pair of white shorts. Also, I was wearing earmuffs. They were green and each muff had a monkey face on it.

"Piper," Mom said, "why are you wearing Erik's old earmuffs?"

"I just feel like it."

Leo kept staring at me as I ate. Then he said, "When are you going to take that thing off your head?"

"Never," I said.

"Well, you can't sleep with earmuffs on," Leo said. He's a year younger than me, but he's sort of bossy.

"Oh, yes I can."

"How are you going to take a shower?" he asked.

I thought about it.

"I'll take baths," I said.

"Who's going to want to be friends with a kid who wears monkey earmuffs all the time?" he asked.

"People who love monkeys," I told him. "Which is everyone."

I tried not to look over at the empty chair. It's the chair that Erik usually sits in. But my eyes have a mind of their own. They peeked.

It was the saddest-looking empty chair I had ever seen.

"Let's get a move on, you two," Mom said. "The boat won't wait for you if you're late."

She had our book bags ready for us by the door. Our life jackets were there too. Mine is an ugly old orange one. Allie O'Malley has a beautiful pink one with white polka dots all over it.

We grabbed our stuff. Mom gave us each a kiss. Then she knelt down next to me and looked me right in the eyeballs.

"You'll have to take the earmuffs off if Ms. Gibbs tells you to," she said.

"Oh, Ms. Gibbs only minds if you talk too much or if you put glue sticks up your nose. She doesn't care about kids wearing earmuffs."

I wasn't 100 percent sure about this.

But I hoped it was true.

CHAPTER THREE

GLUNKEY AND JIBS

At the Peek-a-Boo Island harbor, Mr. Grindle was standing on the wharf next to the *Maddie Rose*. The *Maddie Rose* is Mr. Grindle's lobster boat. Mr. Grindle takes us to school every day. Since only eight kids live on Peek-a-Boo Island, we don't have our own school. That's why we have to ride the *Maddie Rose* to the school on Mink Island.

"Good morning!" Mr. Grindle said to us with a big smile. "How's the wife and kids, Leo?"

"Doing just fine, Mr. Grindle," Leo said.

Leo tells everyone that he is married. His wife is named Michelle and she is a piece of paper. Their children are three yellow Post-it notes that he stuck on Michelle.

"Glad to hear it," Mr. Grindle said, and he patted Leo on the back. Then he looked at me. He squinched his eyes and tipped his head.

"Do you know you have an awful lot of green hair growing out of your ears?" he said to me.

"They're Erik's old earmuffs," I told him. "He gave them to me before he left."

"Ahh." Mr. Grindle nodded. His face was serious. "Today is a good day for earmuffs. They will keep the wind out of your ears."

Leo and I went on board the *Maddie Rose*. The first thing we did was go inside the wheelhouse. That is the little cabin where Mr. Grindle steers the boat. Most of the kids were already in there. They were sitting on the bench, munching on doughnuts and talking. Allie O'Malley was there too. She was not wearing her pink life jacket with the white polka dots. She had on a brand-new one. This one was purple and had mermaids swimming all over it.

"Piper, what on *earth* is on your head?" Allie O'Malley asked.

She talks just like someone's grand-mother.

"It's a baked potato," I said.

"No it's not," Allie said, frowning. "It's earmuffs, with squirrel faces on them."

"FYI, they're not squirrels," I said. "They're monkeys."

"Well, it's not winter, so you look silly," Allie said.

"Yeah, well, you know what you look like?" I said. "You look like Bert and Ernie."

"That makes no sense. I can't look like *both* of them," Allie said. "Plus, I don't look like either of them."

It's true. She doesn't. She's really, really pretty.

On the wheelhouse floor was Mrs. Grindle's basket full of goodies. She owns the bakery on Peek-a-Boo Island. Every morning, she gives Mr. Grindle a basket of something she has baked for all us kids to eat on the way to school. Today, it was doughnuts with powdered sugar on top.

I took a doughnut and went out on the deck. Leo stayed inside with the other kids. Most of them like to ride inside the wheelhouse. Erik and I always rode outside, on the deck, unless it was raining. We loved to watch the water sparkle and to count the lobster buoys. Sometimes we'd spot a seal swimming. Once we even saw a whale.

Without Erik, it wasn't going to be much fun on the deck anymore.

Jacob was out there, too, eating a doughnut.

"Hi, Jacob," I said.

I sniffed him.

"Hey, you don't stink today!" I told him.

"My mom rubbed lemons on my hands," he said.

Jacob's father is a lobsterman, like my dad. Jacob wants to be a lobsterman, too, when he grows up. For now, though, he is the guy in charge of dead fish. All summer long, he goes on the boat with his dad and stuffs dead fish in bait bags to help catch lobsters. The only problem is, he smells like stinky dead fish all the time.

Mr. Grindle started the motor. The lobster boat went *blurble, blurble, blurble*. The next minute, we began to motor out of the harbor.

Jacob and I stared at the water for a while without saying anything.

"Hey, Jacob," I said finally. "See this fellow?" I tapped the monkey face on the right earmuff.

Jacob looked and nodded.

"I'm naming him Glunkey," I told him.

"Glunkey the Monkey," Jacob said.

"Exactly. And the other one"—I tapped

the left earmuff—"I'm naming him Jibs. He can be annoying sometimes."

Jacob nodded again.

He doesn't say much, that's for sure. Sometimes I wonder if Jacob's just pretending to listen while he thinks about lobsters. But then other times, he listens so hard that he can hear things I'm only thinking in my brain.

"Too bad Erik isn't here to eat Mrs. Grindle's doughnuts today," Jacob said.

"Yeah," I said. I took in a deep breath, then sighed. "Too bad."

CHAPTER
FOUR

PRINCESS ARABELLA

The Mink Island School is a little white building with a bell tower on the top. When I got there that morning, kids were already in the playground. I looked for Ruby. She is my best friend from Mink Island. I hadn't seen her all summer because she went to visit her grandmother in New York City. I spotted her coming down the slide. She was wearing a pair of sunglasses that she had hot-glued rhinestones to. On her wrists were about a million homemade bracelets.

I ran up to her, and we gave each other a hug.

"Hi, Thing Number One," I said to her.

"Hi, Thing Number Two," she said to me.

That's what Ruby's dad calls us.

"Hey," Ruby said, "how come you're wearing earmuffs?"

"They're monkeys," I said. I turned my head so she could see Glunkey and Jibs. "Cute, right?"

"O-*kaaay*," she said. She gave me a funny look. Then she said, "Piper, see that princess lady over there?"

She pointed to a lady by the stairs in front of the school.

"Ooh, she *does* look like a princess!" I said.

The lady had long golden hair that made waves all the way down her back. She wore a swishy light blue dress.

"That's our new teacher," Ruby said.

"No it's not. Ms. Gibbs teaches the second-and-third-grade class."

Our school only has fifty kids in it, even though it goes all the way to the eighth grade. That's why they squish grades together.

Ruby shook her head. "Ms. Gibbs moved off of Mink Island. Now we have that princess lady."

I stared at the princess.

She looked nice.

She looked as if she had a tinkly voice.

She looked like someone who wouldn't care if I wore earmuffs in class.

The school bell rang. Ruby put her arm through mine and we hurried inside. We wanted to get seats next to Nacho, the adorable little brown bunny. He is the class pet in the second-and-third-grade room. He's *much* cuter than our classroom pets last year, which were two hermit crabs named Simon and The Other Simon. They were so boring that no one even bothered to think up two names for them.

Lucky us! The seats next to Nacho were empty. We scooted into them very fast. We petted Nacho's soft ears and rubbed the top of his head. Then Ruby and I started to make our Garth Shield. Garth is a kid who makes inappropriate noises all the time. And some of those noises do not come from his mouth. Ruby and I make a Garth Shield at the beginning of every school year. It really works too. We hold hands and close our eyes and whisper softly, "Be gone, Garth. Be gone, Garth." And Garth always winds up sitting on the other side of the room.

The princess lady came in. She stood in front of the classroom, holding a piece of paper.

"Good morning, class," she said. "My

name is Ms. Arabella and I'll be your new teacher."

Ms. Arabella! It even sounded like a princess name.

Princess Arabella.

I smiled at her. I wanted to show her that I was one of those friendly and helpful kinds of girls who also happened to wear earmuffs.

"Don't get too comfortable in your chairs, everyone," said Ms. Arabella.

Uh-oh.

I was very comfortable.

"I will be assigning seats," Ms. Arabella told us.

There was a roar of complaining voices about this.

"Settle down!" said Ms. Arabella.

She did not sound at all tinkly.

Then she made us get up, and she told us where we had to sit for the rest of the year. She made Ruby sit next to Allie O'Malley. And guess where she put me? Right smack next to Garth! He looked at me and smiled. Then he belched, "I like cheese."

I was beginning to get a bad feeling about this princess.

CHAPTER FIVE

PIPER GREEN
(PROPER NOUN)

Ms. Arabella swished up and down the aisles and handed out paper and pencils.

"This morning, we are going to make a class dictionary," said Ms. Arabella. "We will write definitions of ourselves. It will help us to get to know each other better."

She turned around and wrote on the blackboard:

Ms. Arabella (proper noun):

1. Ms. Arabella is 5'6" and has blond hair and green eyes.

2. Ms. Arabella's favorite things:
   painting, teaching, and eating lobster.

I peeked over at Jacob. He looked at Ms. Arabella all lovey-eyed when she wrote "eating lobster."

"Okay," said Ms. Arabella, "now it's your turn, class. If you were in the dictionary, what would it say about you?"

I wrote down:

Piper Green (proper noun):

1. Piper Green has blond hair. It used to be long, but it got chopped to smithereens by her mother, who should not be allowed to cut kids' hair.

I was thinking about my favorite things when I saw some swishing out of the corner of my eye. I looked up. Ms. Arabella was staring down at me.

"Piper?" she said, reading my name on the paper.

"Yes?"

"Piper, earmuffs are not allowed in class," said Ms. Arabella. "Please take them off and put them in your cubby."

"I can't," I told her.

"Why not?" she asked.

I thought about telling her it was "none of her beeswax why not." But I had a feeling that would not go over too well.

"My ears feel naked without them," I said.

Everyone laughed because I said "naked."

Ms. Arabella's face got pink.

"I wouldn't like to send you to the principal's office on your first day of second grade," Ms. Arabella said in her most untinkly voice.

"I don't think any of us would like that," I agreed.

We stared at each other.

Those earmuffs stayed right on my head.

"All right, Piper," Ms. Arabella said, "you will stay in at recess. I will also send a little note home to your parents." Then she swished away.

I stared down at my paper. I told myself

that I would not cry. But like I said, my eyes have a mind of their own. They started watering up. I wiped the tears away. Then I picked up my pencil and wrote:

2. Piper Green's favorite things:
   NOT SECOND GRADE!!

CHAPTER SIX

BOWLING-BALL HEAD

That night, Mom and Dad sat me down for a little talk. Except they were the only ones allowed to do the talking.

"We know you love Erik's earmuffs, Piper," said Mom, "and we understand that you miss him. But you have to listen to your teacher."

Dad folded his arms across his chest. That's what he does when he means business.

"I think it's time to take those things off your head, Piper," Dad said.

I started crying. I wasn't faking either.

Mom and Dad looked at each other. Then Dad said, "Okay, okay. You can wear them until you get to school tomorrow. The minute you walk into that classroom, though, off they come. Got it?"

I nodded.

But a little voice in my ear said, "That's what *they* think."

Sleeping with earmuffs is not easy. Especially if your head is extra round, like a

bowling ball, which mine is. I probably have the roundest head you've ever met.

I tried to sleep on my back, but my head kept rolling

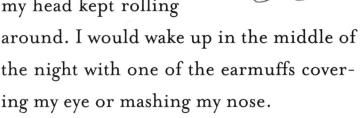

around. I would wake up in the middle of the night with one of the earmuffs covering my eye or mashing my nose.

In the morning, Leo was standing by my bed, staring down at me.

"See! I told you that you can't sleep with earmuffs," he said.

I felt around my face. The muffs were still on my ears, but the fuzzy headband part slipped off my head and hung down around my chin.

"I like it this way," I lied.

"You look like Abraham Lincoln," said Leo.

"He's my favorite president," I said.

I kept wearing the earmuffs upside down all during breakfast, just to annoy Leo.

"Maybe Erik will call today," I said to Mom hopefully.

"I don't know," Mom said. "He'll be pretty busy this week."

I looked at that lonely, empty chair again. Then I gave Glunkey and Jibs each a little pat. Mom saw me do that. She narrowed her eyes at me.

"Remember, Piper," she said, "what are you going to do when you get into the classroom?"

"Take off the earmuffs," I said glumly.

"That's my girl." Mom kissed my nose.

But that voice in my ear said, "These earmuffs are *not* leaving this head."

As Leo and I walked down to the harbor, I worried and worried about the whole situation. Then I had an idea. I don't know why I didn't think of it before.

I stopped walking.

"Oh, oh, *ooooooh*!" I said, clutching my belly.

"What's wrong?" Leo asked.

"I'm sick," I told him.

"You were fine two minutes ago."

"Well, now I'm sick, and I can't go to school," I told him. "I'm going back home."

He took a yellow Post-it note out of his back pocket and held it up to his ear for a second.

"Harold says that if you're faking, Mom will know it," Leo said.

Harold is one of Leo's Post-it children.

"Yeah, well, I'm *not* faking!" I insisted.

I turned around and started walking back

home. Just up ahead, I could see our little gray house. Mom would be very surprised to see me. I began to feel squibbly in my belly. Harold was right. Mom is a nurse. She can sniff out a healthy person like a bloodhound.

I walked more and more slowly. When I reached our front yard, I heard that little voice in my ear again.

This time, it said, *"Hide!"*

CHAPTER SEVEN

GOOD RIDDANCE TO SECOND GRADE

Luckily, I found a good hiding spot right away. It was a tree. Another lucky thing is that I am not afraid of heights. I climbed up that tree, no problem.

It wasn't too foggy, so I had a good view from up there. Our island is called Peek-a-Boo because the fog likes to sit smack-plop on top of us. If you look at us from the mainland, it seems as if our island is playing peek-a-boo, peeping out from behind the fog, then hiding behind it again.

Today, though, I could see all the way to the harbor. I could see the *Maddie Rose*. I could see Mr. Grindle standing on the wharf, waiting for all the kids.

I wondered what was in Mrs. Grindle's basket. I hoped it wasn't cinnamon buns because those are my favorite.

I watched all the kids board the *Maddie Rose*. I watched until the boat motored out of the harbor.

Then I blew a big, spitty raspberry.

"Good riddance to second grade," I said out loud.

Suddenly the door to our house opened. Mom came out. She looked all around. Then she started walking toward the road, very quickly. She was going to pass right by the tree! I sat as still as I could and closed my eyes. I stayed like that for a long time. When I opened my eyes again, Mom was gone.

Phew! Close call.

Then, out of the corner of my ear, I thought I heard something. It wasn't that little voice, though. It was a high, squeaky sound.

I frowned and listened more closely. It was such a tiny sound that it was hard to hear with the earmuffs on my ears. I lifted Jibs up, just a little bit.

I could hear the sound better. It went *whee-whee-whee-whee.* It almost sounded as if the tree was crying.

I lifted Jibs up some more and I put my ear to the tree trunk.

Whee-whee-whee.

Hmm. It sounded as if it was coming from lower down.

I climbed down a few branches. I lifted Jibs up again and put my ear to the tree trunk.

Whee-whee-whee-whee-wheeeeeeeee!!!

Holy macaroni, the tree really *was* crying!

Right at that moment, though, there was a whole other noise. This one blasted so loud that even with earmuffs on, it made me jump.

This noise went *WOWA-WOWA-WOWA!*

I knew that sound very well. It was the fire alarm. After a few minutes, I saw people come running out of their houses. We don't have special firepeople or ambulance people on Peek-a-Boo Island. It's just regular people who help when there is an emergency. I could see Dad out in his lobster boat, racing back to the island. The alarm kept blasting and people kept running.

Boy! I thought. *I miss all kinds of excitement when I'm at school.*

CHAPTER EIGHT

MRS. PENNYPOCKET

The only person who wasn't running all over the place was old Mrs. Pennypocket. She and her brown-and-white bull terrier, Nigel, were taking their morning stroll. Just my luck, though—Nigel decided to go to the bathroom right on my tree.

"Piper?" Mrs. Pennypocket was looking up at me. "What are you doing in that tree?"

"Oh, just enjoying the view," I told her.

"Why aren't you in school?" she asked.

"It's a long story, Mrs. Pennypocket," I said. "Now, can I ask *you* something?"

"I guess so," she said.

"Have you ever heard of a tree crying?" I asked. "Because I think this one is."

Mrs. Pennypocket put her ear against the tree.

"Ayuh," she said. "It's crying all right."

Mrs. Pennypocket stepped on an old stump beside the tree, pulled herself up by a branch, and sat in a wide crook in the tree.

"You're pretty bouncy for an old lady," I told her.

"Thank you," she said.

She knocked on the trunk. Then she put her ear against it and listened. She knocked and listened again. Finally, she hopped back down.

"I need tools," she said. Then she and Nigel hurried away.

A few minutes later, Mrs. Pennypocket came back, with Nigel trotting behind her. Now she was carrying a handsaw.

"Come down out of that tree, Piper," she said.

"Are you chopping it down?" I asked in a shocked voice.

"Just a little piece of it," said Mrs. Pennypocket.

I was beginning to wish I hadn't told Mrs. Pennypocket about the crying tree. Not only did I have to come out of my hiding spot, but now she was going to hack it all up!

I climbed down and sat in the grass beside Nigel. He rested his big, funny-looking head on my lap and sighed. We both watched as Mrs. Pennypocket began to saw at a branch. She sawed for a long time. Every so often, she stopped to fan herself.

"Aren't you hot in those earmuffs, Piper?" she asked me.

"Kind of," I said. Actually, my ears were feeling gross and sweaty.

"Then why don't you take them off?" Mrs. Pennypocket asked as she started sawing again.

"I can't," I told her.

"Why? Are they glued to your head?"

"No. My brother Erik gave them to me."

Mrs. Pennypocket didn't say anything for a minute. She just kept sawing. Then she asked, "Erik went off to high school on the mainland this year, didn't he?"

I nodded.

Since the Mink Island School only goes up to eighth grade, you have to leave home when you turn fourteen. You have to go to school on the mainland and sleep in a dorm or stay with another family.

"Missing him, are you?" said Mrs. Pennypocket.

I nodded again. "Everything is stinky without him," I said.

"Hmm," she said.

Suddenly the branch Mrs. Pennypocket was sawing made a cracking sound. The very next second, it thumped to the ground.

"There we go!" cried Mrs. Pennypocket. "Now climb back up, Piper, and have a look."

I climbed up the tree. When I got to the place where the branch was cut off, I saw something surprising.

"There's a hole in the tree, Mrs. Pennypocket," I said.

"Ayuh," she said. "Go on and peep in."

I peeped in the hole. And guess what? Something peeped back up at me.

CHAPTER NINE

THE FAIRY TREE

I reached into the hole in the tree. My hands closed around something soft and fuzzy. It said, *"Whee-whee-whee,"* but nice and quiet this time. I pulled it out very carefully. It was a tiny gray kitten! It had a pipsqueak of a nose and big green eyes.

"Awww, look at you!" I said, tickling the kitten's chin. "You are as cute as a cupcake!"

The kitten yawned, sticking out its pink tongue. I think it was tired from all that crying.

Then I thought of something. "Hey, Mrs. Pennypocket?" I called down to her. "How do you think this little guy got inside the tree in the first place?"

"Well, sometimes a mother cat will hide her kittens in funny places," said Mrs. Pennypocket. "Maybe the kitten just got stuck in there."

Then guess what happened next.

You'll never guess.

I heard another *whee-whee-whee* from inside the tree.

"Mrs. Pennypocket!" I called out excitedly. "I think there's *another* one in there!"

I snuggled the gray kitten against my chest with one hand while I reached back into the hole with my other hand. My fingers touched something soft and fuzzy again. Very gently, I scooped it up. Out came a black kitten with tiny white feet and a skinny white stripe down its nose.

I lifted up the bottom of my shirt and made a kangaroo pouch for the kittens to sit in. Then, just to be sure, I felt around inside the tree hole to see if there were any more kittens, which there weren't.

I stared down at the kittens in my shirt. They were looking back up at me. I couldn't stop smiling at those cuties.

"You two are like little treasures hidden right inside a tree!" I said to them.

"A treasure in a tree?" Mrs. Pennypock-

et said. "Oh, Piper! Oh my goodness! I just thought of something."

Mrs. Pennypocket hurried away again.

She is a very active old lady, I thought.

A few minutes later, she came back with a cardboard box in one hand and a flashlight in the other.

"Hand me those kittens, Piper," said Mrs. Pennypocket.

Very carefully, I handed her the gray kitten, and then the black-and-white one. Mrs. Pennypocket put them in the box. The kittens snuggled right up in there.

Then Mrs. Pennypocket flipped the flashlight on and handed it to me.

"Now, Piper," she said, "shine the

flashlight down that hole in the tree. Tell me if you see anything."

I leaned over and shined that light into the hole.

"All I see is tree," I said.

But suddenly I did see something. I squinted at it.

"Hey, there are letters carved into the wood," I said. "They say . . ." I squinted harder. "They say L.A.E."

Mrs. Pennypocket clapped her hands and smiled. "I knew it! Those are my gran's initials! Laura Ann Easton. Which means that this"—she gave the tree an excited pat—"is the Fairy Tree."

"What's a Fairy Tree?" I asked.

"It was something Gran told me about," said Mrs. Pennypocket. "When she was a girl, about your age, she found a tree that had a hole in it. It was the perfect place to hide treasures. One day, she put a seashell inside that hole. The next day, the seashell was gone and in its place was a little toy horse. She said the fairies must have left it there for her. The toy horse brought her all kinds of good luck. 'You take a treasure and you leave a treasure. That's how the Fairy Tree works,' Gran told me. I asked her where the tree was, but Gran had left Peek-a-Boo Island many years before, so she couldn't quite remember. She did tell me that she had carved her initials in the hole, though. And here it is!"

"Do I have to leave something in the tree now?" I asked.

Mrs. Pennypocket thought about it.

"It seems like the thing to do," she said.

"But what should I leave?" I asked.

"A treasure, of course," Mrs. Pennypocket said. She picked up her saw. "Look after those kittens, Piper." Then she headed back home, with Nigel jogging along beside her.

I looked at the kittens in the box. They were rolling around and swatting at each other with their tiny paws. I smiled at them.

Things seemed a little less stinky somehow.

I looked for a treasure to put in the tree. First I stuck my hands in my pockets and pulled out an old hair barrette. It was a little bashed up. That didn't seem like a good treasure. I checked my backpack: two pencils, a math book, and a glue stick.

Hmm.

I looked in my lunch box. Tuna salad. *Eww.*

Suddenly I knew just what I needed to do.

Except I didn't really want to do it.

I gave my earmuffs a sad little pat. Then I took them off my head. I kissed Glunkey.

"Have a nice life, Glunkey," I whispered to him.

Then I kissed Jibs.

"Take it easy, old Jibs."

I put the earmuffs into the Fairy Tree's hole.

Right then, I heard my name being called. I looked down the road. A whole bunch of people were rushing toward me. One of them was Dad. He was wearing his shiny orange oilskin pants and his black muck boots. He was also wearing a big frown on his face.

Uh-oh.

CHAPTER
TEN

SPECIAL DELIVERY!

It turned out that when I didn't show up at the *Maddie Rose,* Mr. Grindle had called Mom to make sure I got home okay.

That's when all the fuss started.

"Piper Green!" Dad said in his angriest voice. "Do you realize that half the island has been out looking for you? We were worried sick! Do you know how much trouble you have caused?"

He said a lot of other things, too, which I do not want to talk about. But they included no TV for a month.

When Dad stopped yelling, Mom showed up and she took over the yelling. But when they noticed the kittens in the box, they both simmered down a little. I guess it's hard to be mad with two cutie cupcake faces staring up at you.

"I'm really, really sorry about everything," I told them. "But it's okay now. Because, look"—I patted my naked ears— "I took them off."

"Well, that's a step in the right direction," Dad said.

"Where are they?" Mom asked.

"I decided to give them to the tree," I told her.

Mom and Dad looked at each other.

"Piper, you are a most unusual child," Dad said.

"Yeah, well, Leo is the one who's married to a piece of paper named Michelle," I replied.

It turned out Mrs. Pennypocket's grandma was right. The Fairy Tree really worked! The kittens brought me good luck, because later that afternoon, there was a knock on our door.

"Special delivery!" someone outside shouted.

When I opened the door, my aunt Terry was standing there. She is tall and skinny and she has long, shiny dark hair. She lives on the mainland in a town called Camden, where she has her own beauty spa. I went there once. She painted my fingernails blue and put green mud on my face. I looked like a zombie. It was awesome.

Aunt Terry handed me a bag from a store in Camden. Inside the bag were some cans of kitten formula and two tiny baby bottles.

"Your mom called and told me about the kittens," said Aunt Terry. "Where are they? Where *are* they?"

Aunt Terry is just crazy about cats.

I showed her the box on the floor. Mom

had put a blanket inside the box. She had also put a heating pad underneath the box to keep the kittens toasty warm.

"Awww!" Aunt Terry cried when she saw them. "They are wicked sweet!"

"I found them in a tree," I said proudly.

"Mrs. Pennypocket has been keeping an eye on that tree," said Mom. "She wants to see if the mother cat comes back for them. So far, no mama cat."

That's because it's the Fairy Tree, I thought.

But I didn't say it out loud. I liked keeping the Fairy Tree a secret.

"Oh, by the way, Piper," Aunt Terry said, "I left a little something for you outside."

"Is it green mud from your spa?" I asked hopefully.

"Just go see," she said, and she sat down beside the box to play with the kittens.

I walked to the front door and opened it. There was no package or bag or anything. *Hmm.* I stepped outside. From behind the dogwood bush, someone jumped out and grabbed me.

"Got you!" he yelled.

"ERIK!!!" I started hopping up and down. My face couldn't stop smiling.

He picked me up and flipped me around and held me upside down by my ankles.

"What are you doing here?" I said in my upside-down voice.

"Aunt Terry called to say that she was taking her boat to Peek-a-Boo Island and asked if I wanted to come along. So . . . do you miss me?"

"Nope," I told him.

"Yeah, I don't miss you either," he said, grinning. He lowered me so that I was touching the ground. Then he let me go. I jumped up.

"Come see the kittens!" I said. I grabbed him by the hand and pulled him inside.

Mom and Dad gave Erik hugs, and Mom said he looked too skinny.

"He always looks that skinny," Leo said.

"Thanks a lot," Erik said, ruffling Leo's hair. "How's Michelle doing?"

"I'm mad at her." Leo held up his pinkie, which had a Band-Aid on it. "She gave me a paper cut."

Aunt Terry was sitting on the floor. The kittens were climbing all over her.

"Mom and Dad say we can keep them," I told Erik.

"Now you have to find good names for them," Aunt Terry said.

"How about Indiana Jones and Chewbacca?" suggested Leo.

"Too long," Aunt Terry said. "How about Magnificat and Meatball?"

"Too weird," I said.

And anyway, I already knew what I was going to call them.

The next day in school, everyone's definition of themselves was hanging on the wall. Except for mine.

"I left a spot right by Jacob's for your definition, Piper," said Ms. Arabella. "And it's nice to see your ears," she added, smiling.

"Nice to see yours too," I told her.

She made a little noise in her throat before she swished back to her desk.

I knew exactly how I was going to finish my definition. I had thought about it all yesterday. I picked up my pencil, and in my neatest handwriting I wrote:

Piper Green's favorite things:
My brother Erik, cinnamon buns,
and my brand-new kittens
named Glunkey and Jibs.

THE END

TOO MUCH GOOD LUCK

THE PERFECT STRAWBERRY

I was in a great mood this morning. That was because today Mom was going to paint my bedroom lime green, which is my new favorite color.

"Remember to paint my dresser lime green, too, okay?" I told Mom at breakfast.

"I will."

"And the knobs on my dresser," I said. I scooped up Jibs and put him in my lap. He is my little gray kitten. His brother, Glunkey, was still sleeping on the couch. He's the lazy one.

"Dresser knobs, lime green. Got it," Mom said. She put a bowl of oatmeal down in front of me, and one in front of Leo.

"And paint my bookshelf lime green, too, please," I said.

"Don't you think that's a lot of lime green, Piper?" Mom asked.

"No, because lime green is the best color. It's the color of my cereal milk on Saint Patrick's Day."

"You know why cereal milk is green on Saint Patrick's Day?" Leo said. He leaned over and whispered in my ear, "Because it's leprechaun pee."

I ignored him.

Mom grabbed a bowl of strawberries

from the fridge. She took out a strawberry and began to cut it into my oatmeal.

"Not that one!" I screeched so loud that Jibs jumped off my lap. "That one's got a lump on it."

I am a fussbudget about my strawberries. And the problem with strawberries is that you can almost never find the perfect one. They're either too scrawny or they have dents in them or they have some weird bump growing on their skin.

Mom took out another strawberry.

"I don't like the looks of that one either," I told her.

"Piper, I'm growing gray hairs waiting for you to pick a strawberry."

"I think I see the gray hair," Leo said, squinting at Mom. "It's right on your chin."

Just then, I spied the perfect strawberry in the bowl. It was big and shiny and bright red.

"That one!" I pointed at it. "It's the most perfect one. I love it with all my heart!"

Mom sighed. She fished around in the bowl until she found the one I wanted. Then she held it over my oatmeal and started to cut it.

"NOOOO!"

"Jeezum crow, Piper, what now?" Mom said.

"It's too beautiful to eat," I told her.

ABOUT THE AUTHOR

Although she doesn't ride a lobster boat to work, **Ellen Potter** can look out her window and see islands, just like the one Piper lives on. Ellen is the author of ten books for children, including the award-winning Olivia Kidney series. She lives in Maine with her family and an assortment of badly behaved creatures. Learn more about Ellen at ellenpotter.com.

ABOUT THE ILLUSTRATOR

Qin Leng was born in Shanghai and lived in France and Montreal, where she studied at the Mel Hoppenheim School of Cinema. She has received many awards for her animated short films and artwork, and has published numerous picture books. Qin currently lives and works as a designer and illustrator in Toronto.